Bonjour

Merci

Oui

Chatte

L'amour

This is Elizabeth the cat.

Her mummy calls her
Busy Lizzy.

She has fluffy orange fur,
giant green eyes and she is
always very busy.

This is Busy Lizzy's
beautiful big house.

Busy Lizzy lives here with
her mummy.

Every morning Busy Lizzy
eats a breakfast of chicken
biscuits.

She eats from a silver plate
on a golden table.

After her breakfast she always sleeps on an enormous white bed.

Busy Lizzy is a very happy cat.

When breakfast is finished
Busy Lizzy's mummy goes
to work.

And it's when her mummy is
gone that Lizzy gets really
busy!

The moment the huge pink
front door shuts she is
ready for her adventure.

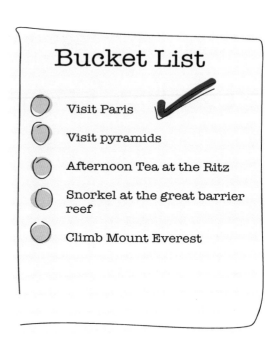

Bucket List

- Visit Paris ✔
- Visit pyramids
- Afternoon Tea at the Ritz
- Snorkel at the great barrier reef
- Climb Mount Everest

Busy Lizzy had been planning her Monday adventure for a long time. On Monday Busy Lizzy wanted to go to Paris.

This would be Busy Lizzy's biggest adventure ever. She would need to get two trains and do a lot of walking.

Busy Lizzy put on her best
dress and shoes.
She left the house through
the big pink front door.

And she took the first train
to London.

On the train she sat by the
window.

She drank a cup of tea and
she ate a tuna sandwich.

Busy Lizzy's second train took her from London to Paris.

It was a full train, there were children, and ladies that shopped and business men.

PARIS

And everyone was happy
and smiling and talking.

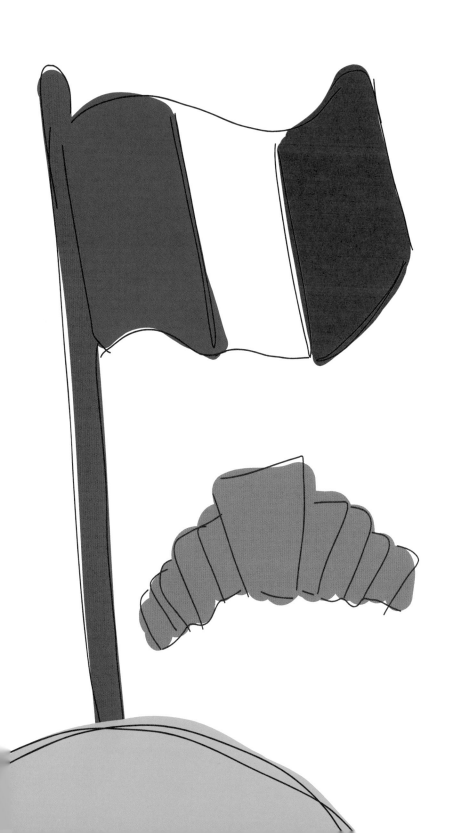

Then all of sudden Busy Lizzy was in the middle of beautiful Paris.

There were so many things she wanted to do.

Lizzy was about to get really very busy!

First she had a cup of
coffee and a pink macaroon.

Then she visited all her
favourite clothes shops.

She bought a scarf, and a
hat and a pair of gloves.

And later she sat on the grass and looked up at the Eiffel Tower whilst eating a picnic.

But before Busy Lizzy knew
it the day was nearly
finished.

Now Busy Lizzy needed to
get home before her mummy!

She made a mad dash for
the train from Paris to
London.

This time though the train
was full of tired people
ready for their homes.

Busy Lizzy was tired.

Busy Lizzy was ready for home.

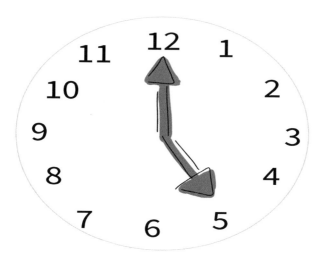

Just in time.

Before her mummy came home from work.

She made it back through the huge pink front door.

She did a big stretch and curled up into a fluffy puffy ball on her white bed.

Perfectly still and ready for her mummy to find her exactly where she had left her.

Bonjour

Merci

Oui

Chatte

L'amour

Dedicated to Alison Williamson

Printed in Great Britain
by Amazon

62919027R00015